SOMEDAY
PERHAPS

Hoping for a change

SARAN RAJ

ISBN 979-8-89026-729-0

SPECIAL THANKS

M. Deepika, Assistant Professor.

Contents

Author's Note

A few days back, I was surfing the internet, and saw a trend dominating the whole social media platforms, 'The 10- year challenge'. People are posting their then and now pictures, pictures of their pets and some places. This 10-year challenge had a lot to do with us. I was excited about seeing the transformation of people over time. To be honest, it was fun to see some transformations. Suddenly, I saw some people posting about global conflicts, global crisis and instability using the same 10-year challenge. Photographs of locations that have lost their aesthetic appeal, pictures of people who lost both their internal and external beauty and some brutal pictures from a terrorist attack.

Yeah, we are aware that, there are both good and terrible things/people holding their breath in this world. But after using deadly force against civilians, killing lots of them, and taking over a country, those responsible were enjoying a swing seat in a children's park. What makes this more nonsense is, on social media most people are normalizing this kind of incident. Making fun of the swing seat incident and stating that "See how child-heartened the terrorists are". Is this how humankind works? - A big no.

Of course, the world has experienced a tremendous expansion in the fields of information technology, multinational corporations, E-commerce and modern lifestyle as of 2023. The sky-scraping growth in e-commerce is literally incredible. With the help of the internet, e-commerce plays a major role in the global retail industry. We're accepting every drastic changes over the years. We know human evolution is a slow process, and some people believe that human evolution has stopped. But the evolution of humans through technology, modern aspects of living, automation, evolving through the internet, is rapidly moving forward. The world is showing fine growth in every possible aspect each and every day. We are just running towards something and we don't even know what we're running for. Why is there a need for humanoid robots when every human is being a robot? With no questions asked, we are just repeating a template for no reason. It's okay to repeat the same template, but we're normalizing a lot of worst things in day-to-day life. We should be happy to have the internet in our lives, But the ratio of internet-based harassment is progressively increasing. What hurts more is, apart from increasing, it is getting normalized. People started making fun of some truly horrible harassment. Ufff, Let's leave this here.

But we're not here to speak or study about industrialization or e-commerce or the substantial growth of MNCs.

So, what is this all about?...

I believe that the majority of the problems that are confronting the world today can only be resolved by children and teens. So this book is all about- a wonderful journey of a young girl and a strange old man trying to be a part of our life and teaching us the best way to live. Apart from listening to everything as a theory, these two characters have some practical observations to afford us. Not only being philosophical, but this book also has a lot for the above problems we spoke about {Normalizing worst things, typecasting, harassment, parenting, mental health etc}.

With little faith in the corner of my heart, I hope this book works.

Chapter 1

Stress to Serenity...

In this world, our lives are quite urgent as traffic on the roads, and Deesha's life is not an exception. A woman in her 28 who is employed as a product analyst in a well-known MNC in Bangalore. Her parents still live in the village where she used to grow up. After a challenging day at work, Deesha returns to her flat, pours herself a glass of champagne and sits on her English rolled-arm sofa. She's been working here for the past five years. Since the first day she was appointed as a product analyst, she had never felt relaxed at home after returning from work. Her school days were the only pleasant days that she had experienced. Because those were the days, her life became more fascinating after she met a strange old man. The strange old man, along with her mom and dad, played a vital role in her childhood. Whenever she gets exhausted due to work stress or feels drained in her personal life, she used to think about those pleasant days. As always, she begins to recollect her memories of those beautiful days that she had 12 years back in her native village. Days that empowered her to be a strong woman and to lead a good life.

The Mysterious Meeting...

It's the mid-90s. That was an amazing evening. The sun was setting down. Birds were returning to their houses independently. All these visuals are running over the eyes of a 68 - year old man, who is lying under a tree. He felt dizzy. He sat up and started staring at the road by rubbing his eyes. It's quite a busy road with vehicles. A group of kids were playing with a ball at the park on his left. He doesn't have any idea about how he ended up there or what happened to him. He had a bag nearby, locked with his hands. It's a brown luggage bag with a quote on its name tag, 'You fly old man- you deserve this'. He was completely blank. He felt thirsty, high adrenaline pumping and a blank mind at the same time.

Suddenly, out of nowhere, a ball hits him on his face. He took the ball and started looking at the bag and ball simultaneously. A kid from the group came nearby to him and pointed her hand towards the ball.

"Give me the ball," asked the kid.

The old man quietly handed over the ball to the kid. Subsequently, the girl began to walk back towards her friends and suddenly, he asked her, "By the way, what's your name?"

The girl turned and started staring at the old man for a few seconds.

"Deesha, My name is Deesha," the girl said.

"Do you know how long I'd been lying here?" asked the old man.

"That's the same question I'm about to ask you," the girl said.

The other kids in the park were getting frustrated and asking Deesha to come quickly. Realizing that the old man was gonna fill her head with lots of questions, Deesha decided to go back and continue her game with her friends instead.

"My friends are waiting," said the girl.

The old man was in a state of confusion and remained silent as he tried to make sense of the situation, while Deesha ran back to her friends and continued to play.

The old man hadn't moved for an hour. He notices that Deesha looks at him at regular intervals. The quote printed on the bag's name tag gave the old man a lot to consider. His parched throat reminded him to find a store nearby, and there was one at the corner of the road. The store appeared to be a pit stop for long-distance travellers. As he made his way towards it, holding onto his bag tightly, he had to pass by the group of children who were playing nearby. They paused and whispered among themselves, speculating about the old man's situation.

"This old man might have been abandoned by his children or he could be a lunatic," they whispered.

However, Deesha had other thoughts in her head. She sensed that the old man needed help. Despite the children's murmurs, the old man made it to the store and sat down on the bench outside, requesting some water.

After drinking a bottle of water, he looked at the bag again. He kept the bottle down and started opening the bag slowly. Suddenly, he heard a voice from his behind.

"Do you remember how you ended up here?" Deesha asked with curiosity.

The old man responded to the girl, "Oh, you little girl again. I still haven't puzzled out why or how I ended up here."

Deesha remained silent because she wasn't sure what to say.

"It's getting dark. Why are you still here? Reach your home soon," the old man said.

"Yes. But have you thought about how to find food and shelter for tonight?" asked the girl.

The old man chuckled and said, "I don't know about food, but I'm not gonna have a luxurious stay tonight."

Deesha quickly thought for a moment and then extended an invitation to the old man, saying, "Alright, come with me."

"Where?" the old man asked.

"My mom always cooks delicious food. You should try some," the girl said.

The old man, who was feeling quite famished, eagerly agreed to accompany her. That's an empty road filled with a few street lights. The old man was walking behind Deesha as she darted around on the road.

"Wouldn't your mom scold you if you suddenly took a strange old man to your house?" asked the old man.

"No." Deesha replied.

"How can you be so sure about that?" he asked.

"A few years back, I brought Chaachu to my house. My mom hadn't scolded me for bringing her home. That's how I'm sure now." - Deesha said.

"Who is Chaachu?" he asked.

"She is my friend."- Deesha said.

"That's why your mom hadn't scolded you." - the old man replied.

"No, that's the first time I saw her. When I was heading back home from the park, I saw her standing all alone on the street corner. Something in me prompted me to approach her, and I took her to my house, but my mom didn't scold me for it," Deesha said.

"Fair enough. How long should we walk to reach your home? I'm hungry," the old man asked.

"It's just two more streets away. What do you have in your bag?" Deesha asked.

"I don't have any idea about what's inside, it just feels like some clothes. I was yet to open it, but the sky was getting gloomier. So better I could open it after sunrise," replied the old man.

Deesha doesn't know what else could she possibly ask him. Her only thought was, she felt an inexplicable connection with him, like they were old friends. Upon reaching her home, Deesha rushed in to tell her mother about her new friend. To her surprise, her mother welcomed the stranger with a smile and invited him inside.

"Your house seems pretty good." the old man said.

"Do you still remember the way your house looked?" she asked.

The old man had a chuckle and said, "I haven't lost everything in my mind. All I just lost is a little part."

Deesha's mother served the old man a plate of rice and roasted fish.

In her curiosity to know about him, the little girl started questioning him a lot about his situation. He smiled and responded to each question she asked, despite the fact that her questions were pointless and ruining his supper. After completing his dinner, the old man left the house and thanked Deesha and her mom.

He came to the place where he woke up this evening. The trees shredded their leaves a lot. He kept his bag down and started cleaning it. After cleaning those leaves, he lay down and looked up at the sky. He saw something unusual in the sky and began to concentrate on it. A moon with no stars is all he can see. He really can't remember the last time he saw the sky this way. The muscular urge to open the bag was making the old man think a lot about it. But he was literally tired and felt a lot sleepy. With his eyes closed, he murmured to himself, "To figure out what is happening, I must remain calm and composed." After a while, he eventually fell into a deep sleep.

The sun rose again. Leaves were falling from the trees; birds were back - flying for the survival of the fittest. He is enjoying these aesthetic views. He looked for the girl and other kids in the park. But the park was empty as his head. He thought it might be a good idea to open the bag now. So he started walking towards the store, sat on the bench, took a deep breath and opened the bag slowly. There was a paper rolled up and tied with a blue ribbon inside. A couple of clothes and a balanced amount of money were kept in. After slowly removing the ribbon, he started reading it.

"Hey old man, you awake? How do you feel now? I was your authorized caretaker for the past three years. It's been difficult for us after you had a head injury and experienced momentary memory loss. Days turned into months, and months turned into years in your recovery phase. You have recovered quite slowly for the past three years. Once you have completely recovered, you had desired to start everything afresh. As you wish, start from a new page. Don't worry if you fade out or lost in the situation sometimes. It's common for you. We kept a couple of clothes and some money which belongs to you. I wish I could see you again old man, Bye."

He started rolling the sheet, tied it up with the ribbon again, and kept it in his bag. He finally finds out how he ended up under a tree, but he has no idea about the person who wrote this letter. He agrees with this situation because this situation was absolutely created by him. He took a while to spend the time quietly and later got some food from the store to fill his tummy.

He started observing the environment. It just looks like a small village and there weren't so many people around. He needs to find a job and a shelter to stay in. He spent the rest of the day thinking about himself and looking for Deesha.

As he wished, Deesha came again to the store to have a look at him. "Where were you the whole day?" asked the old man.

"Kids are meant to be in school on weekdays," said Deesha.

"Have you never been to school, old man?" she asked.

"I had," the old man replied.

"I have been thinking about you the whole day at my school. Have you found out how you ended up here?" she asked.

"Yeah, I had. But you know what, I've been looking for you since early this morning. Are you making your way here directly from school?" he asked.

"Yes, I am," - Deesha replied.

The old man feels like he got a new friend here. Both started having a fun-filled conversation. The old man thinks that having a conversation with this little girl sets his heart and mind free.

* That's how everything works, right? There is always a possibility that we may get stuck in a loop, or when we can't cope with some losses, we need someone or something to set us free. Mostly it's not something. It's "someone." A person who can make us feel better or just to say - "it's alright."

"Tell me about yourself," asked the old man.

She smiled and asked him, "What do you want to know about me?"

"Anything about you is okay," the old man replied.

With a floral smile, she asked him, "Anything or everything?"

"Whatever you feel comfortable saying, you can," the old man replied.

I am 16 now. This village is where my grandparents used to live. I've been living here since my childhood. My dad works in a chocolate factory which is located on the north side of the village. My mom takes care of the calves and goats we have. Every day, I follow a fixed routine that involves going to school, returning home, and hanging out with my friends. Even though I detest going to school, my dad always makes me go. Whenever I tell my dad, I'm not interested in going to school, he starts his favorite dialogue, "It doesn't matter whether you're learning or not, just go enjoy your school life. So I can easily spend my hand-full of money [his earnings]".

My mom and I often make fun of my dad for his handful of money jokes.

You know what, he struggles with expenses for the house with the little bit of money he earns. He feels like, I don't want to know about his struggles.

"That's how fatherhood works, right?" she asked.

The old man had a smile on his face at her mature statement about fatherhood.

"This is what I am all about," Deesha said.

"What can you tell me about yourself?" she asked him back.

"It's a long story; you don't have much time to listen," he replied.

"My parents aren't home, so time is not a concern. I'm all ears," Deesha said.

"Why," he asked.

"My mom isn't feeling well, so my dad took her to the hospital," she replied.

The old man took a deep breath and started to explain about him.

As same as you, I was born in a small village too. I haven't got the privilege of having good parenting. My parents were literally busy with their business and personal issues. I grew up being a reserved person who only experienced loneliness and anxiety. High school and university life were good, but I'm not good at making friends. To be honest, that's not my kind. I aspired to learn law at some good university, but life had some other ideas for me.

On the other hand, I didn't have any people to let my sorrows out and started walking alone on the streets. When you keep everything inside your heart and fail to express your emotions, that's nothing but a dead weight.

After a period of time, I met a woman who really cared for me a lot and it felt like, life was somewhat beautiful after her arrival. But with that kind of life (with depression and anxiety), I was completely introverted. So even when she gave me lots of love and care, I failed to provide her with the same. But she never gave up on me. She thought standing with me in my most challenging time was the greatest thing that she could ever do for me. That's what she is.

Spending countless hours talking to each other was something we used to do frequently. Things went quite well. Unexpectedly, she met with a fire accident and the wounds on her face were worse. She lost her glow on both her face and heart. It was really the hardest time of our lives. We spoke a lot again. We spoke about the recovery process and, I took care of her quite well. But she had some other plans. She used to tell me that, she couldn't bear the pain. Just after a couple of days, when I returned home after a grocery purchase, I saw her lying on the floor. I felt something wasn't good and took her to the hospital real quick.

But she was no more.

She waited for me to leave the house so that she could execute her suicide plan. After that particular incident, life pulled me back to where I really belong (Those bleak and solitary days from my past). I took on the guilt of being the cause of her demise. I should have been more attentive and caring towards her. I was just completely lost and standing all alone again. Can't even move an inch in life after that particular incident. At the same time, I got sick too.

A year later, my dad left this world with a silent goodbye. Life is so cruel. Medication to my sickness, her absence, and my dad's demise never let me have a comfortable nap. I thought getting a job could really make me move on in my life, but India is a country where unity in diversity lies only in words. India is divided into several things like caste, community and belief in god. It's acceptable to hold these beliefs, but it's unfair to discriminate against other people based on these beliefs. There are still many franchises here that hire only their own caste people for white-collar jobs. I'd been treated worse in a private franchise based on caste. I mean really worse.

I resumed wandering alone on the streets, just as I had before. At the same time, my health too got worse. Undergone surgery, either which also hadn't worked well for me. I suffered from post-operative complications.

Years passed. I started a restaurant with the little bit of money I had and life gave me a second chance as a discount. Another woman, another love story. This woman is a guardian angel for me. She was two years elder than me, but we didn't use to care about it. She gave me a lot of comfort to every inch of my heart. She changed me.

We got married. It's been 32 years of our married life. Life went pretty smoothly, but not mentally. The memories of failures, losses and those traumatic events never made me feel comfortable. The only antidote that helped me to overcome that phase is nothing but my wife and restaurant. We turned old. She too passed away a few years back. That's why I chose this journey I think. I need some more time to recall everything that I forgot. That's it. – The old man said.

"It's really sad to hear all of this. How can someone go through all these phases? Anyway, what's your name?" Deesha asked.

"I'll tell you later," the old man replied.

"You have lived with all these worse moments in your life. What's your opinion about life? or tell me something to learn about," Deesha asked.

"Life is not something that you can completely learn from books or movies or from someone's advice. Perspective towards life differs for each individual. Books, movies and some people's advice may help you, but you can't execute everything in your life from that. So you've to overcome a period of time which takes years and years to learn about life. The struggles you go through over a period will make you understand what life is," the old man said.

"But apart from teaching you about life, I can tell you about some topics which need to be learned by everyone," said the old man.

"What's that?" Deesha asked.

We all live in a kind of thought that things that keep happening to us are meant to happen and we named it fate. Yeah, fate is a part of life, but we can't blame fate for everything that happens to us. For 70% of things that happen to us in our whole life, we are the complete reason for it. Our lack of effort and our thoughts towards those things will make that worse. Things that happening around us are cruel sometimes. We just move forward with putting up a sad face while hearing those cruel things. We can't stop those cruel things completely by just snapping our fingers. But with a little faith, we can use the weapon called "CHANGE".

We're overcoming a series of events that were poised with both good and bad. With a lot of melancholic things happening in this world, do we have any role in making this world a better place to live? Yes, a bit. - the old man said.

"It's not possible to observe and fix the world when we have a lot to do in our personal life," Deesha said.

When a nuclear weapon hits the ground, it may inflict damage up to 30 kilometers on its surrounding from the point of impact. In such a way, changing a few things in our day-to-day life and having a change in our thoughts from childhood can make things better. The impact of a change in thoughts will redefine the way of our lives and lead us in a good way until we die. Along with making our lives good, it'll reshape the thoughts of people around us too. From how we raise our children to how those children face this society. If teenagers change, so will the following generation. Creating a change in the lives of children begins with providing them with a positive and comfortable environment through good parenting. Let me give a clear understanding -the old man said.

Parenting is An Art

In this busy world, work stress and emotional pressure are making our mental health worse. Our busy schedules often make it challenging to spend enough time with our children. Most parents aren't differentiating their personal environment and professional environment. Some people resume their professional work at home even after leaving their office. Having work pressure is okay, but kids have nothing to do with this. All they expect is our valuable time & our love towards them. Some parents hand over the television remote/mobile phones to their kids. Television and mobile phones can be a part of life, but do they learn life from television/mobile phones?

The suicide rate among teens is rising high. And in other cases, kids suffer due to their parent's ego clashes and misunderstandings. In this current generation, it's a thirty-seventy ratio. Thirty percent of parents were really taking care of their kids well. Seventy percent doesn't. We failed to teach the good things to our kids & failed to shower enough love on them. Like the growth of a plant, it's a process that takes time. If we need our kids to grow up well, we have to afford them enough time, love and good parenting. Before providing good parenting to the kids, parents should know about what good parenting is.

There is an outdated belief in society that parents who are educated or those who reside in cities are offering excellent parenting to their children. But good parenting is not based on cities, rural places, or the modern lifestyle. It's all about the maturity, experience and mindset of parents. Parents need to take a moment to pause from their hectic and fast-paced lives in order to enhance the well-being of their children. Spending quality time and having healthy conversations with children can help them to develop an improvised opinion about society. -the old man said.

"Can you make it easy for me to understand?" Deesha asked.

"Okay," he replied.

Bruno Versus Us...

Let's imagine you're sitting alone in a park, and at 40 meters away, there is a dog standing in front of you. It has a dog tag on its neck with the name Bruno. Bruno is looking somewhere else and he doesn't have any idea about you. After a few minutes, he started barking at something else and you too don't have any idea about what he is barking at. He smelled the chairs placed near him and started moving away slowly while continuing his barking. He was heading towards the gate to get out of the park. But you had already picked up a stone and were ready to throw it at Bruno. He doesn't know you have a stone in your hand. Will you throw at him or not? - the old man asked.

"Yes, I'll," she said.

"Okay, would you throw the stone if there was a tiger or a wolf instead of Bruno?" the old man asked.

"No," she said.

Yes, you won't. Exactly, this is what I'm talking about. Bruno is not against you & he doesn't know you have a stone in your hand, and he is not in the idea of attacking you. He was heading towards the gate, and he is never going to think about you hitting him. Then why should you want to throw a stone at him?

Because the fulfillment you get from completing the process of hitting him will make you feel satisfied. So, without a thought or a conversation in our mind, our brain conventionally makes us throw a stone. Not everyone is gonna throw a stone, but 70% of people do. Why do most people want to hit Bruno or other people, who cannot defend themselves? This is called obsession with winning. Everyone is obsessed with winning.

The world has changed everything and everyone in a competitive way. A conversation about competition, success and failures should take place between parents and children. More importantly, we have to teach them how to face failures. Only failures can teach everyone about what they are capable of. After leaving home, children face everything in a competitive perspective. There is always a competition for them in schools. So the only place they feel comfortable is at home. That's why good parenting needs a lot for them. -the old man said.

"So I don't have to be competitive with others. That's what you're saying, right?" Deesha asked.

"I'm stating that, you don't have to contend with everyone or everything. Just concentrate on the area where you are strongest," the old man said.

"What is the point of competing in only one field?" Deesha asked.

Yes, you're right. This is where good parenting comes into play. There is a huge difference between competing and learning. You have the absolute freedom to learn everything that you're interested in. But you don't have to compete in everything that you learn.

For example, if you have a strong aptitude for music, you can work hard to succeed in that field. While fighting for music, you have the complete freedom to learn whatever you wish to learn. After succeeding in music, if you want to compete in other skills, you can. But without being the strongest contestant in any particular field, why do you wanna interfere and compete in everything? -the old man said.

"I get it," Deesha said.

"Good. There is a reason behind my statement," said the old man.

"What's that?" Deesha asked.

People nowadays believe that suicide is their primary choice after a failure. The suicide ratio among teenagers is rising. As I already said, I'm not gonna afford any advice about life and how precious life is. But failures and losses are okay. Instead of committing suicide, everybody should know about their goals and what they need to compete at. Parents should teach their kids about their goals, respect other people's emotions, and not to typecast others. - the old man said.

"What is typecasting?" she asked.

"Typecasting means people strongly believe that aggressive people are criminals even if they haven't committed any crimes. Similarly, a person who is seen as quiet might be typecast as a loner or outsider," he said.

"Is this what typecasting is?" Deesha asked.

"Yes. Let me complete the remaining," the old man replied.

Parents should make their kids grow with clarification on what to win and what not to. First of all, parents should have a level of maturity in their life to teach their kids about every good things. It is acceptable to be competitive in terms of what we need, but we don't have to win each and every competition in our lives. Apart from having a conversation about being competitive and successful, parents should speak to their kids about every possible topic that they can understand. Most of the people and parents in this world are stuck in social conditioning. Most parents are driven by the societal conditioning mindset to compel their children to strive for victory in all aspects of life. On the other hand, parents force their kids into something without their interest because that's what society likes to see. When everybody pulls social conditioning from their mind, life could become much more beautiful and fulfilling to live.

"So I shouldn't care about the people in this society?" Deesha asked.

"No, you've to be socially helpful to others without becoming socially conditioned to unwanted things. You don't have to push yourself or others into something which this society wants to see," the old man replied.

Parents must develop their own sense of morality to teach their children what's right and wrong. This way, their children can also learn to think about ethical issues on their own. Not only about being competitive, parents and teachers should teach kids to stand against discrimination. As I already said, most people say discrimination is dead. But we can surely be able to see students in universities form a gang and follow this casteism & racism things. In our day-to-day life, we read newspapers, magazines and on the internet that school kids, college youngsters, and guys in the workplace bully their co-people. Where do they learn to bully others over race/caste/religion?

Some people say that there is no more discrimination over casteism/racism things are happening in this world. How dump it is?

Parents should speak to their children about all of these subjects in an ethical manner.

So the first step in making this world a better place to live is being a good parent and affording good parenting to the children. That's the major thing if we're looking for a change.

"There is a word that always leads us in both good and bad ways, 'FOLLOWING' the path," the old man said.

"What's wrong with the following?" Deesha asked him.

Disparities By Birth...

"My wife once narrated me a story about society and people. Even after losing some of my memories, I still remember that story," the old man said.

"Apart from listening to your advice, I'm more interested in your mid-conversation stories," she said.

"I'll take that as a compliment." -The old man replied with a smile.

"Go on. I'm so curious to listen," she said.

"Do you have any idea about Yeti?" The old man asked.

"What does that mean?" she asked him back.

"Deesha, Do you actually go to school? Tell me, where do you go all day?" the old man asked.

Deesha was taken aback by his question, and in a hushed tone, she asked him, "Why are you asking me like that?"

"Then what, whatever the question I ask, you just come back with a question to me about 'what that means', replied the old man.

Deesha laughed and urged him to start the story.

"The Yeti is a mythical creature that resembles an ape with a body full of white fur," the old man said.

"So, the Yeti wasn't a real life-creature. It's a cartoon, right?" Deesha asked.

"No Deesha, many people believe that Yetis existed in the past. However, till date there is no scientific evidence for Yeti's existence," the old man replied.

"Okay. Continue the story," Deesha said with curiosity.

The Yeti's Melting Point…

There is a village on the top of the mountain which was ruled by a king named Fakir. The people who live in that village have no idea about the outside world. The king and the people in the village were so happy in their lives. As they live on the top of the mountain, they have no other problems except the winter season. During the summer season, they form into multiple gangs and split their work. One will hunt for food, and the other will collect dry wood for the winter season. The rest of the people in the village will do farming. This is their life routine.

Days passed, and winter has arrived. The extreme cold due to the high-altitude environment is a challenge for them during winter. The snowfall has brought a white landscape to the area outside the huts. So everyone in the village is supposed to stay inside their huts. During times when it snows, the king regularly visits the village once a week to make sure the people's needs are met. The winter hasn't troubled them a lot for the first few days. But a week later, in the early morning, a man from the village came out of his hut and set up a campfire in front of it. He sat there and started feeling the warmth of the campfire by enjoying the snowfall. Suddenly, he saw a white-furred creature hiding behind the tree. He doesn't have any idea about what he is looking at. That creature is just looking at him by hiding behind the tree. For him, that looked like a kid covered in a white-furred dress. When he started focusing on that creature's face, he got afraid and ran back into his hut. He told everything to his neighbours about this incident, and surprisingly, his neighbours also said the same to him. They all discussed about it and decided to tell their king, Fakir. As they wished, the king came to their village the next morning. The King was sitting on his horse, and soldiers were surrounding him. The king commanded the soldiers to gather the community in the middle of the village. -the old man said.

Because of his non-stop talking, the old man began to cough.

Deesha took her water bottle from her school bag and asked the old man to have some water.

After drinking some water, the old man asked Deesha, "Can I continue the story tomorrow?"

"This story is lot more interesting. Don't stop," Deesha said.

The old man started looking at the surrounding. There weren't any people on the road, and the place was so silent. Some of the street lights were flickering, but the multi-color lamp in front of the store made the scenario an aesthetic one. He stood up from the bench and came in front of Deesha, and told her that he would mono-act the rest of the story to make her enjoy it even more.

She was so excited and asked him to resume the story.

The old man started continuing his story;

After a few minutes, everyone in the village gathered and surrounded the king. The king could clearly sense that something was not right. So in a louder tone, he asked everyone, "Tell me what made you all look so frightened?"

A man from the village raised his hand and said, "Your Highness, we saw a white-furred creature hiding in the woods, and it was focusing on our huts. We had never seen anything like that before, it appeared to be a miniature monster."

King Fakir was wordless and appeared to be striving to recollect something. He had a memory of his dad talking about Yetis. So he asked the people, "Does it look like a snow monster?"

"Yes, but a small one." - the people chorused.

So, he ordered everyone to remain in their huts and not to step out until it was necessary. He promised them that his soldiers would guard and monitor the village, and as he said, he left some of his soldiers there and returned to his palace. After having some words with his ministers, he passed an order to build a strong cage with a lot of spears on top of it. As per his order, they started building a strong cage with iron bars and wooden spears on it.

On the other side, the following morning, this small Yeti was sleeping in the woods and snow covered all around her.

Deesha stopped the old man and asked him, "she?"

"Yes, it's girl Yeti. Like you," the old man smiled and continued the story.

Neither the king nor the people had an idea about the snowfall because everyone was afraid of Yeti and interested in locking her in a cage. Yeti realizes that the snowfall is increasing every day, and it's going to destroy the village.

As she does every morning, she got up from the snow and headed near the village. She hid behind the tree and started staring at the huts. Indeed, her focus was not on huts, it was on the flames. The flame on the campfire was all she was focusing on. Yetis reside only in the snow zones, so the beauty of flame draws her in. She was attracted to it, and her eyes were filled with the visual of flame. Some kids in the village were playing around the flame and showing their hands towards the campfire to feel the warmth. After seeing all these visuals, this little girl Yeti wishes to join them. But she has a fear of those people and the guards. She sat down under the tree and remained mesmerized by the visual of the flame.

But the people and King Fakir had other ideas about Yeti. They increased the pace of building a cage, whereas the snow was deposited up to the foot.

One night, Yeti was hiding behind the tree and the flame was seducing her a lot. Without any hesitation, she started stepping towards the village. She went near a hut, sat in front of the campfire and looked at the flame closely. It seduced her. She tried to point her hands towards the flame as the kids did earlier. Suddenly, a soldier who was walking behind the huts saw a little monstrous foot mark on the snow. He followed it and saw her sitting in front of the campfire. Without having a thought or conversation in his mind, he conventionally threw the spear toward her. He knocked on the doors of nearby huts and asked everyone to come out. The spear he threw missed the Yeti, but she was afraid of both spears and the guards. Some people stayed inside the hut and watched this through the window.

Yeti was frightened and saw the guards throwing the spears toward her. In the urge to escape, she stepped into the campfire and fell into it. She was born and lived all her years in a snowy field. The heat from the campfire was making her struggle. She woke up and ran into the woods again.

The news had been passed to King Fakir. He had arrived at the location with his ministers and soldiers, and after a while, he ordered the soldiers to bring the cage and instructed them to light up a campfire inside it. King Fakir knows that flame is the major thing that makes Yeti come. But people don't know why the king asked to place a campfire inside the cage. He ordered his commander-in-chief to reduce the number of soldiers on guard and returned to his palace.

After running into the woods, Yeti started rolling on the snow. She couldn't resist the pain, so she took a handful of snow in her palm and applied it to her burns. Her eyes were filled with tears. She kept applying the snow for hours and hours.

She is aware that the snow's been piling up each day, and in a week or two, this place will be buried. Her thoughts were on the flame again. But leaving this village and migrating somewhere is the best thing for her. So she chose to go back and spend some time with the flame before leaving the village and migrating somewhere else. She went to the tree where she used to hide before and sat behind it. The flame mesmerized her and made her walk towards the flame once again. But this time, it led into a cage.

She did everything right to get into a cage, without anyone noticing. Guards are not the issue this time, it's the doors. The doors were locked and she didn't know about that. She sat inside the cage and started enjoying the flame again. Hours passed and a guard saw this. In a fraction of a moment, everybody in that village gathered in front of the cage. The news had been passed to the king.

Yeti was afraid and ran near the doors. The people and the guards around the cage were throwing spears and stones inside the cage. She doesn't have any idea about what to do. If she runs towards the door, they hit her with spears and stones. If she walks to the middle of the cage to avoid spears and stones, the flame hurts her. Due to heavy snowfall, King Fakir's arrival has been delayed. So some people around the cage decided to climb upstairs and dismounted the spear lock. Guards were watching these scenes casually, and the spears had been dismounted. Those sharp spears on the top of the cage started falling inside and pricked Yeti's body. With her body full of spears and bleeding, Yeti closed her eyes by seeing the flames. - the old man finished the story.

"Is she dead?" Deesha asked.

"Yes. What kind of question is this?" asked the old man.

With a low tone, Deesha asked him, "Does the king come?"

"My wife hasn't said me about that. Anyway, what is the point of coming now?" he asked

With a sad face, "In what way does your wife match the context of this particular story with society and people?" Deesha asked.

"I know you're disappointed with the end. Do you really want to listen to the moral?" asked the old man.

Deesha just shook her head up and down.

The old man began to tell the moral.

The villagers had no clue why the king wanted a cage or why he told them to set up a campfire inside the cage. In a similar way, the majority of the people in this society are unaware of the origins, reasons, and basis behind the caste system and various religious beliefs. There are a lot of theories behind the origin of the caste system, like traditional theory, racial theory, political theory, occupational theory and etc. The traditional theory says that the caste system is an extension of the varna system, where the 4 varnas originated from the body of Brahma. The Head, arms, thighs and feet of Brahma. It raises the question of why a god would create such differentiation and discrimination between people by assigning one from the head and another from the foot.

According to political theory, the caste system is a clever idea invented by a particular caste people in order to place themselves on the highest ladder of social hierarchy. While the other theories carry different stories.

"In the formation theories behind the caste system, I agree with Dr. Ghurye and Sir Herbert Risley that "Caste is a product of a race that came to India along with Aryans". Because this theory makes sense." the old man said.

Coming back to the topic, In this system, people adhere to notions of high and low, oppression of certain groups, varying standards for different social classes, and other similar beliefs.

Not just one person in this world is a Yeti. Every individual, including you and me, will experience a Yeti-like state at some point in our lives. For everyone in this world, there will be longing and competition over a lot of things like desire, dreams, ambition, life and love. Just as the Yeti was making her way towards the flame, all of us were running towards our desire, dream, ambition or love. So, if we're running towards those things, there must be two choices at the end of the tunnel. One is winning on it, other is losing. While winning or losing may doesn't matter, it is crucial that one's success or failure should not be determined or influenced by their caste, community, religion, or race.

What more could you do if you have exerted every effort to succeed in your journey, but have been unsuccessful due to discrimination based on caste, community, religion, or race?

We are the Yeti and the people who live at that top of the mountain are the society that surrounds us. Like King Fakir asked to build a cage, Aryans created the caste system. The caste system created inequality. The caste system or different religious beliefs might be good for most, but the inequality it created was the major issue here. Deesha, keep in mind that cages serve a dual purpose of safeguarding both those outside and inside of them. -the old man said.

Deesha shook her head and the old man continued.

For now, the people in the village killed Yeti. But the ongoing snowfall will eventually kill everyone in the village. In a similar way, we too will die someday of aging or some unanticipated events. If there is a beginning, there must be an end at some point. We're not aging backwards Deesha. Even if we do, we'll end up where everything started. No matter how deep and deep you go towards the start or the end, there will be nothing but a void waiting for you there. In the midst of all this, what do we gonna achieve by discriminating, hurting, and body shaming others?

Like sheep in a herd, we are divided into various groups, and most of us are sprinting forward to discriminate against others. Aryans created the caste system on the basis of employment and occupation. The objective of the caste system is for the succeeding generation to carry on their father's occupation. That motive has been changed nowadays and everyone has the right to do whatever job they wish. But where does the discrimination come from? Why is it still here?

Aryans created it for some reason and evil-minded people manipulated this system in a different way. There are two ways to understand the discrimination we face in society. Firstly, when the Yeti attempted to escape, it got hit by spears and stones. Similarly, we encounter discrimination from many individuals in society. Secondly, like the Yeti battling the fire in the middle of the cage, we experience emotions such as pain, anger, and depression when we are humiliated or discriminated against.

The ability of humans to fulfill their desires and needs is what sets them ahead from animals. Even after stepping into the fire, Yeti wished to spend some time with the flame again. In the same way, it's an individual's choice to choose what they want. The only difference is that the Yeti only has an affinity for fire, while humans have a fondness for a lot of things. Similar to the Yeti who was slain while hoping to spend some time with the fire one last time and depart from the village, there were lakhs of Yeti's (Humans) who had died and their dreams have been shattered. Their longing had a tragic end, for hoping a better life somewhere on earth with their loved ones, desired job, or victory in a competition.

Like the people who saw Yeti die through the window, many of us are just watching everything that happens in society.

"Deesha, there are no such things as disparities by birth. Remember that," the old man said.

"So there is no way going back in this topic," she asked.

"Do you want people to change?" he questioned her.

"Why not?" she questioned him back.

We always follow a track that has been laid in front of us by our ancestors. Some of those things were good; some were really bad. It's totally foolish if we ignore everything. But what we have to think about is, why most of us are so obsessed with Caste, Community, Religion, Race, Borders, etc. Why did our ancestors choose to prior these things over humanity and equality? The major reason is the lack of education. Parents have to teach their kids to oppose these things. The initial step should be for parents to object to such things.

The origin of humankind is Africa, and we all know that. The human evolutionary process led to the emergence of HOMO SAPIENS. When human evolution was in the early process, the only struggle that people went through was for food. Fighting over food was a common occurrence for them. During that period, there was no hatred or separation based on race, caste and religion. People began to become economically stable as the population grew rapidly, and the concept of "status" emerged. It's a personal choice to improve their status. But discriminating against others by their status is not a healthy thing. 80% of people really don't know about the formation of the caste system, what it is used for or why we still follow it. However, their understanding is that caste, community, religion, or race are the criteria to stereotype or discriminate against someone.

It doesn't matter whether you're good or bad; it doesn't matter whether you're educated or not; If you're not in their particular caste/religion/race- they don't value your growth, your love and your character.

In recent times, most people have started to change their mindset, as everyone is equal. But the ratio of people who change is not equal to those who remain unchanged. - the old man said.

"Last weekend, my friends and I headed towards the park. We saw that the park had been locked and we don't know why. So we made a choice to get back to my house. A vast expanse of empty land lies behind my house, and a portion of it belongs to my dad. We have a farm for our cattle there and I don't know about the remaining. So we chose to go play on that empty land behind my house. While we were running around aimlessly, my mother suddenly emerged from the house and instructed us not to cross a specific boundary. We agreed and resumed playing. A few hours later, after my friends were gone, I ran back to my home and got refreshed. As my mother was busy preparing food, I asked her the reason why we shouldn't cross the designated boundary. However, my question went unanswered. After my dad came home, I asked him about my mom's statement. My dad said that we're not supposed to go in there because that land belongs to the upper caste, and we're restricted to go," Deesha said.

"The old man has no answer to tell her about that." So he remained silent.

"So this is what you're talking about, right?" she asked.

"Yes."- the old man replied.

"Go on," she said.

Don't believe if people say we're in a caste-less society or everyone is united. Start reading newspapers, till date there are N number of news about discrimination can be seen.

The main reason people being in this dirty pit is due to social conditioning. Wherever you go, whatever you try hard to flourish, social conditioning and typecasting will be there to break you. If you haven't faced any of these things till now, Come On, You Haven't Even Started facing this Society yet! Like the immense growth in technology, harassment and discrimination through the internet is also rising high. It's hard to see people with good hearts losing everything due to discrimination. You know, still there are lots of places following untouchability in some countries. Religious, social, and racial are the factors of untouchability. People make their kids learn that being distant from a particular group/race of people is normal. Does that mean we are the king?

We will never be!

It's Okay to Be...

Can all these things be renewed and changed? Can we live in a world where there are no borders?

Maybe not now. We don't know what the future is gonna bring us. It's like tossing up a coin. We tossed up, and the coin is flipping in the air. It may take a considerable amount of time before we can witness the effects of the next generation and its impact on society.

To Be Honest, it's okay to have borders between countries and different religious beliefs. But discriminating, oppressing, and humiliating others is not acceptable. Whatever it may be, whether you're a religious person or an atheist, keep everything to yourself. Never bring that into public. Never form a gang in an educational institution where kids learn or in the workplace.

Overcoming any form of discrimination can be challenging, but there are a few steps that can be taken to cope with its impact. Focusing on our strengths and seeking support systems to manage emotional, physical and behavioral changes are important. To prevent discrimination or harassment, it is important to decline any involvement in such activities, steer clear of offensive humor or practical jokes, and familiarize oneself with workplace policies. If you encounter situations where your workplace or superiors encourage such activities, it is imperative that you take a stand against them.

There are numerous legal avenues to pursue in order to take action against discrimination or harassment.

Deep down in the heart, let's think twice before letting out those criticizing, discriminating and racial statements about others. – old man said.

Like a coin has two sides, the ones who bully others just move on to their next target, but the ones who got bullied get stuck in that situation for a long time. They struggle with the chaos inside their head. When people go through bullying, losses, failures, and traumas, they will get mentally hurt. Apart from failures and losses, being in a toxic environment is one of the worst things which can make us mentally drain. Leaving away from the toxic environment is the best way to process self-love and feel worthy. - the old man said.

"I know what mental illness looks like," Deesha said.

The old man started laughing and asked the little girl, "How?"

"When I was a kid, my mom used to take me to school every day. While we were heading to the school, we often saw an abnormal woman sitting alone with her hair messed up, torn dress and speaking with herself. That woman always had a cat with her. She used to roam everywhere in this village, but I don't have any idea about where she is now. When I started going to school on my own, my mom once told me not to have a conversation with that woman. I asked my mom, Why? She said that woman is a lunatic. That's how I got to know about mental illness." -Deesha said.

The old man continued to smile and said, "There are lot of differences between being a lunatic and having a mental illness. As you said, that abnormal woman on the street might be insane, but you can't typecast everybody as insane who has a mental illness. Even the most beautiful people can also deal with mental issues. There are various types of mental illnesses in this world. Some will affect our physical health if it's left untreated. This is quite an important topic, I'll explain," the old man said.

The Quiet Struggle with Chaos of Mind

Mental health is always a serious topic that has never been noticed or taken immense action about it. Only some people and some countries do, but I was literally speaking about the majority.

In the lives of human life infrastructure, there will be losses, failures, and tragic events, and they will surely haunt us for a particular period of time. Some people have the ability to cope and overcome the phase quickly. Some can't cope for a really long time. As we go through those tough phases of our lives, our mental health will take a drastic toll. Our mental wellness will suffer, depending on the intensity of the crisis we're facing. There are multiple layers of processes to overcome those phases, like the grief process, coping with the loss, etc.

When you ask someone to list some physical diseases, they will list out a lot. But when you ask them to list out mental illnesses, most people can't say more than 2 or 3. Mental health and mental disorders have a separate universe that deals with basic issues like depression & stress, to some serious disorders like PTSD, Bipolar, Schizophrenia, OCD and etc. Each and every disorder has different phobias to deal with. TBH, most people believe that, like soda to chest pain, keeping ourselves busy is the best way to get rid of mental health issues. Coping with the losses takes time. So yes, the first thing to get out of mental illness is to keep ourselves busy. But we should not handle it on our own when we start to face sleeping disorders, headaches, auditory hallucinations, flashbacks etc. - the old man said

"This is the first time I'm hearing about the seriousness of mental health, and it's surprising me," she said.

"Really?" the old man asked.

"Yeah, I already have some knowledge about previous topics, but mental health is completely new to me," she said.

"But, I can't explain a lot about mental health. As I already said, mental health and mental disorders have a separate universe," said the old man.

"Why isn't enough education on mental health in schools?" she asked.

"I don't know, but having an education about mental health in schools can make the kids know about self -love and etc," said the old man.

"You overcame a series of tragic events; have you suffered with this?" Deesha asked with hesitation.

"Yes, I am," the old man replied.

"So you have a remedy for it?" Deesha asked.

With a soft smile, "I don't have any remedies. Seeking medical help, diagnosing, valuable therapy, and having emotional support is the best option. But I can tell you something about what we should do from our side and how society should handle it," the old man said.

The old man continued to explain to her,

It is common for people to have conversations with themselves in their own heads. How does that really impact our lives?

All of us will eventually have a conversation or an argument with people we know in one way or another. But the comfort we get while having a conversation with ourselves has no match in this world. Because it will often lead us to believe that our points are valid. Sometimes it might be a good point, while sometimes it's not!

As I already said, most people in this world, including us, typecasting everything/everyone without our knowledge. As same as that, the majority of people have the stereotype that those who have mental illnesses are lunatics. That's why many of them are not letting out about their mental illness. In other scenarios, people don't even know how to explain their issues. The stigma surrounding mental health is preventing people from seeking help. The lack of knowledge regarding mental health is the root cause of all of this. So, having a good education about mental health is the first thing to overcome mental illness.

Our mentality of "what we think is always right" needs to be changed. That's the best way to stop typecasting. If the typecasting stops, the ratio of people who let their voice about their mental health issues will gradually rise. If it's raised, the mental health issues will be normalized. Each and every single human being has their own problems to deal with. It doesn't matter whether the problem is big or small. When we go through a hard phase in our life, it really makes our mindset a tricky one.

Till now, the seriousness of mental health has never spread completely. As I said, most people never know they're suffering. Nearly a billion people are suffering from mental illness officially around the world. We never got to know about the remaining. That tricky mindset we go through makes people addicted to drugs, suicidal thoughts, aggressive thoughts, sleeping disorders, personality changes, stepping back from the real world, etc. -The old man said.

<u>What Do We Have to Do?</u>

The best and possible way is to get psychological help, therapies and emotional support. But there isn't enough awareness among people, and there is always a lack of time for us to have that.

Surely we need to take a look on it at some point, but this is all about us and what we have to do.

What we have to do is, BEING GOOD to others. We see people all around the world criticizing and discriminating against others through social media and in real life. We have to take a step to stop it. Let's avoid laughing at things by criticizing others. This is not about particular aged people. This is apart from age restrictions. We all are covered in it. If someone is mentally alone, depressed, left alone, going through losses or failures, all we have to do is listen to them and make them feel comfortable. Making them feel like they're inside a warm blanket on a hard cold day is the greatest thing we can do. The chaos they listen inside them has no words to explain. Tell them that's normal. If it's a serious one, recommend having a therapy. But if we can't do these things, let's be silent and step away.

If we criticize those who are not well, we're also the ones in their books and we can't run away from our own chaos. That will surely shrink our faces. Let's love them or leave them.

We all have/had peaceful days, looking at the leaves falling from trees as the soft music travels through the air. Let's give them that or let them hear on their own.

"We can speak a lot about this, but having a wide education on mental health is the only antidote for this," he said.

"I can't get it exactly, but I can understand mental health is a serious thing to care about," she said.

"Yes."- said the old man.

"Time passed real quick. Come let's get some dinner," she said.

"I found some cash in the bag this morning. So I'll buy food here," he replied.

"After you left my house yesterday, my mom and dad had a conversation about you. He asked me to bring you home for dinner. Seems like, my dad needs a favour from you," she said

"What kind of favour does your father need?" the old man asked.

"I don't have any idea about that. But he asked me about you and where you belong to," she said.

The old man started thinking about it for a few seconds and asked the girl, "What did you tell your dad about me?"

I said, "I saw that old man lying under a tree near the park and he didn't have any idea about how he ended up there. Both my dad and mom had a conversation about you for a few minutes and later on, he came to me and asked me to bring you tonight."

The old man agreed with Deesha and both started walking to Deesha's house. "So what's your parent's name?" the old man asked.

"When I asked about your name, you haven't said anything. So, first, tell me yours," Deesha asked.

"I said, I'll tell you later," he replied.

"Then I'll tell you later too," Deesha replied in a arguing tone.

"Come on Deesha, how could I address them without knowing their names," the old man said.

With a disappointed face, "Tilak and Sradha are their names," she replied.

"Thanks," he replied.

"Keep your thanks to yourself until you give your name," Deesha told in a frustrated voice.

The old man laughed.

After several lectures, they silently made their way back to Deesha's house.

Deesha's dad welcomed the old man.

Both of them shook their hands and the old man asked Deesha's dad, "How is your wife now sir?"

"We will speak about that later. Let's have dinner first," Deesha's dad said.

Four of them sat down and started having dinner. Everyone was silent and Deesha's dad seemed sad. The old man noticed that Deesha's mother did not appear to be in good health. She looked exhausted and depleted. So, to make the place normal, he told Deesha's mom that the food was tasty. But as he expected, there was no reaction from anybody except Deesha. As usual, Deesha turned and started to question the old man about his past. But he stopped her and said, "Please no more questions today".

Deesha laughed and continued her dinner.

After completing his dinner, the old man came out of the house and washed his hands. Deesha's dad was standing in front of the door and the old man went near him to thank.

With a lot of hesitation, Deesha's dad asked the old man, "Can you do me a favour?"

"Sure sir. But what kind of favour?" the old man asked.

"Stop calling me 'sir', you can call me Tilak." -Deesha's dad said.

The old man said "Okay", and started listening to him.

Yesterday, my daughter told me about you and your situation. I'm not sure if it is appropriate to request this favour from you, but I feel that you are the best person I could ask for help. - Tilak said.

"Just tell me what I should do for you," the old man asked.

Tilak hung his face down, with full of melancholic feelings in his heart he told the old man, "My wife has been unwell for the past few days. So, we visited the doctor today."

"Is anything serious Tilak?" the old man asked, as he was concerned.

Tilak's eyes were filled with tears. The old man held Tilak's hand and asked him again, "What did the doctors say?"

Suddenly, Deesha came out of the house to listen to their conversation. Tilak saw her coming towards them, but he don't want her to see him with tears. So he turned towards the old man and told Deesha to go back in. After she ran back into the house, Tilak told the man, not to share this situation with Deesha.

The old man promised Tilak and asked him to tell about his wife's situation.

Tilak wiped his tears and told the old man, "She is been suffering from Arrhythmia".

Arrhythmia? asked the old man, to know about the disease.

Tilak's eyes were filled with tears again and he explained to the old man about his wife's medical condition.

"In a simple term, she is having irregular cardiac rhythm," Tilak said.

"Don't get this thing into your head Tilak, she will be alright soon," said the old man.

"That's what we both were hoping for," Tilak replied.

"What help do you need from me?" asked the old man.

"With her medical condition, she can't really take care of everything around her," Tilak said.

"Yes," said the old man.

With a little bit of hesitation on his face, Tilak asked the old man, "Deesha told me about you and your situation. If you don't mind, can you stay on my farm and take care of our livestock?"

The old man was thinking about it and he can't say no to Tilak.

"You are in a difficult situation with no house to reside in and no place to go. So, if you're okay with taking care of the calves and goats, feel free to stay here as long as you like," said Tilak.

The old man took some minutes and said, "Okay, I will."

"Thanks a lot. After knowing about her condition, I really got stressed about managing things. I'm really grateful for your help. Thanks again," Tilak said

"It's fine. You don't have to thank me again and again," said the old man.

Tilak notices that Deesha was standing near the door, So he came closer to the old man and asked him not to tell Deesha about her mom's condition. The old man promised Tilak that he will never tell this situation to Deesha.

"Where is your farm?" asked the old man.

"It's just a kilometer behind the house. We'll go there and settle up things for you," Tilak said.

Both of them went near the door and Tilak asked Deesha to bring the torch. Deesha was searching for a torch and the old man asked Tilak, "Have you told Deesha that I'm staying on your farm?"

"I doubted whether you would agree to stay or not. So I haven't told her about this," Tilak said.

Deesha was bringing the torch towards them and asked Tilak, "Why do you need a torch now Dad?"

"Your new friend is gonna stay with us. He will take care of our farm and cattle," Tilak said.

She was so surprised and asked him, "Do you really gonna stay with us?"

With a smile, "No I can't stay with you and answer your dump questions about my past, so I'll stay on your farm," said the old man.

Three of them laughed about the old man's joke and Deesha asked her dad, "May I come with you to the farm?"

Tilak agreed with her and asked her to wear her slippers. As three of them started walking, Deesha came near the old man and said, "I'll introduce Chaachu to you."

"Okay, bring her to the store tomorrow after school. We'll spend some time with her," said the old man.

"No, we'll meet her now," Deesha said.

With a doubtful facial expression, the old man asked her, "Now?"

"Yes. Now," Deesha said.

What do you mean Deesha, it's getting late at night. How could we visit her at this time?- asked the old man.

"We're on the way to meet her," she said.

While Tilak's been listening to all of these conversations, Deesha was doing her best to get the old man to believe her, but the old man assumed Deesha was joking about Chaachu. She came near the old man and said to him, "I'm not kidding, you've to believe me."

"We're heading to your farm and how's she gonna be there?" asked the old man.

Deesha and Tilak started laughing at the old man's question. The old man got frustrated and asked Tilak, "Come on Tilak, you too joined with her?"

Deesha couldn't stop her giggling, and the old man got even more frustrated. Amidst her giggles, she told the old man, "I'm not lying, I'm being honest with you. She is in the farm."

"You're telling me that she stays on your farm with your cattle and she doesn't have a house to stay in or parents to care for. Right?" - asked the old man.

"Yes. Of course," she said.

The old man was confused and he didn't have any idea about this. He had a look at Deesha and Tilak and both of them were laughing continuously. He lost his patience and posed them with a lot of questions, "You're confusing me. How is it possible? How can you make your friend stay on your farm all day? How can she not have a parent or a house? How did your mom leave you without scolding for suddenly bringing her home and making her stay there?"

Tilak and Deesha both burst out laughing at the old man's questions, making him feel like the crazy one. He decided not to ask them anymore about Chaachu.

"Enough Deesha, don't make him mad," Tilak said.

But she couldn't stop her giggling and told the old man, "I promise you, I'll introduce her once when we reach the farm".

"Okay," said the old man.

Three of them reached the farm and Tilak got the torch from Deesha and went near the door to open it. The old man stood near a tree and started looking around. There were some trees around and he could feel the breeze. There was a handwoven bed near the tree with a pillow and a folded bed sheet. There isn't any sounds from the cattle, so he felt, he could sleep peacefully. At the same time, Tilak opened the door and asked the old man to come.

"First of all, ask her to bring her friend Chaachu. We'll look for other things after that," said the old man.

Tilak put up a smile on his face and Deesha ran into the farm to bring Chaachu. The old man was looking at the door for her arrival while Tilak's been arranging the stuffs on the farm.

Deesha came out of the farm and told the old man, "She is sleeping, do you wanna wake her up?"

"Yes. You promised me that you would introduce her to me after reaching the farm. So bring her," the old man said.

She ran back inside the farm and after a few seconds, she bought a goat with her. She was laughing hard and Tilak was smiling at this situation. The old man knows he was fooled by Deesha. With a disappointed smile, he asked Deesha, " Is this your friend Chaachu?"

By controlling her giggle, Deesha said, "yes".

"Come on Deesha, you took me to your house because you were confident that your mom didn't scold you, when you took Chaachu home. Right?" the old man asked.

Deesha nodded her head up and down with laughter.

With a smile on his face, the old man told Deesha, "What if your mom thought me as a kidnapper or a lunatic? I was happy that your mom haven't hit me with anything."

Three of them had a banter for a while and Deesha left Chaachu inside the farm. Tilak told the old man to take care of himself and he would meet him later. After having a fun filled hours, both Deesha and Tilak made their way back to their house. The old man walked into the farm, carrying his bag, and it was a fair-sized farm.

It's clean enough, and there isn't much livestock there. Just a few goats and two calves. He can't drop his bag on the floor. So, he looked for a shelf, but there weren't any shelves inside the farm. He thought, if he could find something resembling a hook, he could hang his bag on it. He started searching for it, but despite his search, he couldn't find anything like a hook. So he stepped out of the farm with the plan to hang his bag on a broken branch of a tree, where the handwoven bed was placed below it. After hanging the bag, he sat on the bed and took a deep breathe. He lay on the bed, and he got plenty of thoughts crawling on his head.

He may have been teasing Deesha, laughing and giving her his advises, but he felt an emptiness somewhere inside him. He doesn't know where the feeling comes from, but he felt it all around him. Amidst all the chaos, he couldn't ignore the inner void he had. As he was lying, he saw the sky and it looked different compared to last night.

Same as last night, he began to focus on it, and he figured out the difference. That's a star. Last night there were no stars, and he can spot one tonight. It was near to the moon and looked beautiful too. The soothing breeze of the air filled him with a calm feeling, that made him eventually fall into a deep sleep.

The sun rose again. He got freshened up and changed into new clothes. He decided to look out for a hook and he couldn't find any. Instead of looking for one, he decided to make one on his own. There were lots of broken branches and he could make one from them. So he started walking to Deesha's house to get some carpentry items.

He approached the door and knocked on it. Sradha (Deesha's mom) opened the door and asked the old man about his needs.

"Is Tilak here?" asked the old man.

"No, he has gone to work," Sradha replied.

"I thought he would be at home. So I can borrow some carpentering stuffs to make a hanger and shelves for the farm," the old man said.

The old man gasped and told her, "It's okay, I'll be back in the evening."

"He works on double shifts these days, so he returns home late at night. I'll look for it if you let me know what you need," said Sradha.

"Just some iron nails, a drill and a saw," he said.

She went in and took a while to get those things. The old man waited for her and after she bought those stuffs, he asked her, "How is your health?"

"It continues to remain the same, not getting worse or improved," Sradha said.

"Don't fret; it will get better," he said.

She remained silent, and after a few seconds, she told him, "Hope so."

The old man could clearly sense that she appeared to be exhausted. So in order to avoid discussing about her health, he asked her, "Is Deesha already gone to school?"

"Yeah. Her exams begin today. So she'd left earlier," Sradha said.

With a bit of hesitation, "Are you comfortable with staying and taking care of the farm? I told Tilak, not to disturb or cause any inconvenience to you," Sradha asked him

"Absolutely, it's completely fine. You can put your worries aside and not to worry about that," he said.

"Tilak made sure you weren't left out and made breakfast for you too. As long as you are staying with us, you're supposed to dine here. You don't have to feel hesitant," Sradha ordered him with a smile.

"Yeah, sure," he replied.

"I will be right back with your food, just give me a minute," Sradha said

The old man took the stuffs necessary for the carpentry work and accompanied them with his breakfast, and headed back to the farm.

Once he had finished his food, he took those cattle from the farm and tied them under a tree; Leaving some water for them.

He started collecting some broken branches and wood and began to work. After a few hours of carpentry work, he crafted some hooks and hangers and hammered them inside the farm. He thought, it was just a hook and hangers and it won't take long to craft. But it took hours to get the exact thing he wanted.

He approached the handwoven bed, which was placed beneath the shadow of the tree. He sat there for a while and started having thoughts about this farm and his work. It isn't a hard job to do. He simply brings the cattle from the farm in the morning, feeds them some grass and water and ties them under a tree. During the sunset, he should bring them back inside the farm and provide them with water and grass. This is his routine. It was quite boring for him, but he can have a lot of rest.

He finds himself unable to escape the sudden void inside him from last night. Whenever he used to have some issues like this in the past, his wife devoted herself to taking care of him and ensuring his well-being. His mind wandered back to the days of his life spent together with his wife. Although he lost his memories of several days due to that head injury, he was still able to recall a few days. Reminiscing some of the special moments between them, he began to blush with nostalgia. Some gave him tears.

All of a sudden, he heard someone behind him. It's Sradha and she was bringing him his lunch.

"I thought you'd come to grab your lunch. But you didn't show up. That's why I got it myself," Sradha said.

"Oh I'm sorry, I should've told you. I usually skip lunch. I only partake in breakfast and dinner. I'm sorry again," said the old man.

With a smile on her face, she told him, "It's fine. Have your lunch today. We'll skip it from tomorrow."

He began having his lunch and Sradha left, telling him to come home for dinner. Time went pretty slowly, and he took a nap under the shadow.

When he woke up, its almost sunset and he freshened up by washing his face and took the cattle back inside the farm. After completing the protocols for them, he took those carpentry items and started walking towards Deesha's house.

He expected Deesha, but its Sradha again who opened the door. He gave all those stuffs and asked about Deesha.

"She went to her friend's house to work on exam preps. I think Tilak will take her with him on his way back home," Sradha said.

As he began eating his dinner, the aroma of fried potatoes wafted through the air, making his meal all the more enjoyable.

With thanks to Sradha for the dinner, he headed on his way back to the farm. As usual, in his routine, he went under the tree and lay on the bed. He turned his attention to the sky and could spot a few more stars than the previous night. But the void inside him remained the same. The inner emptiness drives him towards nihilism and a feeling of aimlessness. At the same time, as the stars rise in the sky, they seem to communicate a message to him. With a multitude of emotions, questions and musings swirling within him, he eventually drifted off to sleep.

Chapter 2

A week had passed, and he had been following a monotonous routine, doing the same job every day, and sleeping for the rest of the hours. He either receives his food on time or goes to get it himself. On every occasion that he went to Deesha's house for dinner, he couldn't spot her at home, and therefore, decided not to disturb her during her exams.

The extreme of being alone makes a profound effect on him. Both the inner emptiness and the stars in the sky were gradually increasing day by day. He started exploring the concept of loneliness and hope at the same time. He had a hope that if he spent some time with Deesha, it would make him feel better. So he went over to her house and knocked on the door.

When Sradha opened the door, his disappointment was a consequence of his high hopes.

"Is Deesha home?" asked the old man.

"No, it's her last exam today. Last night, she was telling me about her plan to meet you this evening. So she will be at the farm after school," Sradha said.

Upon hearing this, the old man felt great and asked for some cleaning supplies and headed back to the farm. As his usual routine, he started completing the protocols that needed to be done for the cattle and farm. He settled down under the tree to have some rest till evening.

The Void and the Glimmer of Hope

The sun was getting to the horizon, and he started doing those monotonous evening protocols to cattle. When he came out from the farm finishing those works, he saw Deesha coming towards him. He made his way to the tree and took a seat under it. Soon enough, Deesha joined him and sat beside him.

"It seems like it's been days since we met," Deesha said.

"Yeah. A week," he said.

"How did you do on your exams?" he asked

"Ah, pretty good. But not up to my dad's expectations," she replied.

"Hahaha. I was looking for you at your house at dinner, but you weren't," he said.

"Yes. I was with my friends. Anyway, how has the week gone by?" she asked.

With an exhausted expression on his face, "To be honest, it's been a rough one," he said.

"You seem a little upset. Does this place have something to do with your mood? You can tell me if you're uncomfortable staying here," she asked.

The old man's face contorted into an awkward expression, and Deesha can sense something is wrong with him. Continuing to keep his face in an awkward reaction, he said, "No, really not. Yes, but uh…."

"You're literally blathering," she said.

"No, I don't have any issue with staying here. Even if it's boring to be here all day, I'm happy to get more rest," he said.

Deesha was a lot worried about seeing him disturbed by something. "So, what's bothering you?" she asked.

He remained silent as his inner emptiness makes him feel disconnected from the present. As written in his letter, he started fading out a bit. Deesha was questioning him repeatedly, but nothing fell to his ears because of his mental chaos. She tapped his shoulder and asked him, "What's bothering you?"

"I'm confused," he said.

"What confuses you? You seemed like an expert in all matters of life a week ago. I'm surprised to see you confused," she said.

He remained silent and started looking up at the sky.

"What do you see up there?" the old man asked in a subtle tone.

"Sky, stars and a moon," she said.

"No. There is something you can't see up there," he said.

Deesha was confused about his statement and said to him, " You must be kidding."

"Nope, I'm not," he replied.

"Then what's up there? I can't see anything apart from stars and the moon," Deesha said.

"That's what I'm disturbed about," the old man said.

Deesha noticed that his face appeared lifeless, and she was expecting him to share about his situation. As she expected, he started to rant about it.

"Have you heard about the ancient Chinese philosophy of Yin and Yang?" he asked.

"Nope," she said.

"You could have seen that, but you don't remember it," he said.

"What does it look like?" she asked.

"The two halves of a circle, one half was white, while the other was black and both were intertwined with each other. Black represents Yin and White represents Yang. Both black and white have a small circle within them, which is filled with the opposite colour. Like a small white circle in a black half and a small black circle in a white half," the old man said.

"Yeah, I've seen it. But I don't know about its philosophy," she replied.

"Yin symbolizes darkness and negativity, while Yang symbolizes light and positivity. The two halves are not separate, but rather they are interconnected and dependent on each other. The small circle within each half represents the seed of its opposite, stating that each principle contains the essence of the other. This represents the idea that everything in this world has its opposites and is interconnected," he said.

"In the same way, after going through much tragedy in my life, I feel like I'd arrived to the world of void. At the same time, these stars in the sky were giving me some hope. let me explain," he said and continued to explain his situation.

I'd lost so many people in my life and some were really tragic. As we spoke a week ago, it doesn't matter we age backwards or upwards, there is nothing but a void waiting there for us. There is something inside me, that makes me feel emptiness all around my heart.

The concept of void differs from each perspective. In Eastern philosophies, there is a saying that the void is an essential aspect of existence that allows us to let go of attachment and desire. However, this idea of the void can also be seen as a source of anxiety and despair in Western philosophies.

Considering my situation and the way I see things, this inner emptiness makes me feel hopeless and leads to despair. This is not the first time I'm facing a situation like this, but this time it feels more difficult to handle. At the age of 68, I'm left wondering what else I can do to overcome this void. People often suggest moving on is the best way after a loss or event, but in my case, there seems to be nothing to move on to.

On the other hand, it's the stars. The day we first met, I went back to sleep under the same tree where I had woken up. I looked up at the sky and I couldn't spot any stars in it. But the very next day, the count of the stars was increasing slowly. However, with each passing night of the week, the number of stars gradually increased. Every night, it felt like the sky was telling me stories and filling me with hope.

Yeah, it works this way. Whenever we go through a hard phase or some loss in our lives, the very next day, life continues to move forward with or without our wish. Even the simplest things like a gorgeous sunrise or blooming flowers can make us feel the beauty of hope. It reminds us that life is not just about the losses we've experienced, but also about the moments of joy and love that are yet to come. Even when it feels like everything is falling apart, if we wish to hold on to hope, the light will guide us through the darkest of times.

On the other hand, it's okay to choose to let go of hope and live without it, but it's crucial to be aware of its effects on our life and mental health. If we opt to take this path, it's essential to keep our thoughts free of mental chaos. Ultimately, it rests on our shoulders whether we choose to proceed with it or not.

It's perfectly normal to have a sense of emptiness within you at some point in your life or to feel optimistic about the future. But what happens when you experience both at the same time?

In my situation, the Yin Yang philosophy holds true, where both my emotions contain the essence of each other. Like having an inner emptiness for the whole bright day and hope from the stars even in the darkest of nights. Balancing both at the same time leads to a complex mix of emotions in this situation. Feeling despair, hopelessness and hope at the same time is the wildest combo of emotions. - the old man said.

"So, how can you overcome this?" she asked.

"I am not sure, to be honest. A few days ago, I was reminiscing about my wife and the happy times we shared. If she is still alive, this phase would not be a concern," the longing in his voice was reflected on his face as he said.

Deehsa was wordless as she was concerned about him. Hoping to bring a smile to his face, she teasingly said, "It's true that having loved ones closer can make you feel better, but at 68, who's gonna come forward to marry you? You might have a hard time finding someone."

The old man began to laugh out of his heart and both of them kept grinning for some time.

As he kept laughing, "I've no plans to get married again," he said.

After a short silence, Deesha asked him, "So there is no possibility of getting through this phase?"

"Knowing the purpose of our existence can help alleviate feelings of emptiness," he said.

"Then find it," she replied.

"That's a complex process and challenging, but if we find it, it provides a sense of fulfillment that can't be found elsewhere," the old man replied.

"So what's stopping you from finding?" she asked.

"That's a complex process," he said again.

"What complex?" she questioned him.

"Deesha, I'm mentally tired and have lost interest in seeking redemption or overcoming this phase. All I can do now is just exist as a stubborn rock under the ocean," he said.

"Merely existing? That might make you even more bored," she said.

He had a smile on his face and said, "While it may not seem exciting, there's something intriguing about simply existing."

"It sounds like you're shifting to a fresh topic of discussion," she said.

"Why? Is it boring?" he asked.

"No, your conversations are always interesting to hear. But it is getting dark. So let's make this as a final topic of the day," she said.

"Yeah. Sure," he said.

The Enigma of Existence

There are countless mysteries and questions in the world that remain unsolved. Like the disappearance of Amelia Earhart, DB Cooper's case, the Bermuda triangle, the Voynich manuscript and even the origin of the caste system is a mystery. At some point in our lives, we've all been asked the age-old question: which came first, the chicken or the egg is also a mysterious question.

There are a lot of theories and beliefs behind every question and unsolved mysteries. What makes life more interesting is experiencing, discovering and understanding the mystery behind this. In a similar way, after the rise of humans, one of the mysterious questions that left unanswered is, what is the reason for our existence? Why are we here? What is the meaning of life? While there may never be a definitive answer to this question, the search for meaning is what makes life so beautiful and precious.

"At the same time, it was a complex process, as I said," he said.

"What complex?" she questioned him back.

"As I said, finding the purpose of our life can give us fulfillment. But at the same time, there is an equal possibility of going deeper into the void while finding it," he said.

"How can it do both?" she asked.

"There is no one exact answer to the question of what the meaning of life is, as it differs for each individual. But when you start chasing on finding the meaning of life, you'll mostly end up with two common answers. Some people believe that the purpose of life is to seek happiness, while others contend that life is a loop and we should relinquish our desires and acknowledge the illusory nature of the people, relationships, and possessions around us. So if you started believing that everything is illusionary, you'll get deeper into the void and feel like life is completely empty," the old man replied.

Deesha understood what the old man said, and asked him, "At least you should try to cope with the situation, even if you feel like, it was pointless."

"Yeah, that's why I don't want to find the purpose of life or try to escape the void. The moral of the enigma of existence is not a problem to be solved, but a mystery to be embraced. So apart from fixing all this and finding the purpose of life, I wish to just exist and wonder about the mysteries," he said.

"If that keeps you mentally fine, you can," she said.

He let out a sigh and said, "Let's see what comes."

"Have you had your supper?" he asked her.

"Nope," she said.

"Go home and have your dinner. It's getting dark," he said.

Deesha went inside the farm and had a quick look at Chaachu, then bid the old man a good night and headed back home.

After Deesha left, the old man continued to sit beneath the tree and felt the cold breeze. His thoughts were surfing about his late wife, void, hope and Deesha. Overcome with mental exhaustion, he eventually fell asleep.

Chapter 3

Months passed and it's been almost a year since the old man's arrival in this village. He can clearly notice that everything around him has changed except his monotonous routine. Deesha's school life is nearing its end, Sradha's health is getting better, and Tilak started working one shift per day. The inner void he experienced became familiar to him. Deesha visits the old man every weekend, and their bond gets strengthened with each visit.

One fine day, Deesha came to the farm at dawn with a sad face. The old man was doing the protocols for the cattle and he saw her sitting under the tree. He took a while to finish his works, freshened up and sat beside her. He asked her how the day was gone, but she remained quiet.

"How was your day?" he asked her again.

"Worse," she said.

"What happened," he asked.

"I had a misunderstanding with my parents," she said.

"Tell me clearly," he asked.

"My final exams are gonna end in a few days. I was asking my parents to take me to the town for higher studies. But they are not interested in letting me go. They want me to study here in this village," she said.

"Why are they not comfortable in letting you go?" he asked.

My dad feels like he wants to be with my mom during this phase. She was getting better day by day, but he wanted to be with her during this process. It might take at least 6 hours to travel to town and a parent or a guardian needs to be there for the paperwork. So it might take at least 2 days. That's why he is worried about leaving Mom alone.

"What's his final decision?" the old man asked.

"He asked me to wait for a year or consider taking some other courses nearby. He promised me that he would take me to the town for my studies next year," she said.

"What did your mom say? Is she too against you?" he asked.

"Nah, she is my side," she said.

"What have you decided?" he asked.

With disappointment and anger in her tone, "Nothing to decide. I can't wait for a year," she said.

"If it's okay for you, I'll speak with him," he said.

"No use of it. I can understand his situation, but I can't waste a year. He accuses me of being disrespectful whenever I try to explain the significance of this year to him," she said.

The old man remained silent and started listening to her situation. He began to empathize with her and asked her a few open-ended questions. So that she can express herself further.

"Do you really speak in a disrespectful way?" the old man asked.

"If speaking the truth and facts means disrespectful, yes, I am," she said.

The old man was stunned by the answer and said to her, "Yeah, many people may feel discomfort with truth, but it's equally important to remain calm while communicating," he said.

"So what do you say, "Even if I'm right and I've valid points, should I remain silent to prove my respect?" she asked.

"If you have valid points and truth on your side, it doesn't matter its your parents or a stranger, you have to stay tight and fight for it," the old man said.

"Let me tell you an incident," she said.

"Yeah, go on," he replied.

The Balance of Courtesy

"From childhood, I grew up attending the same school, but something changed over the last three years - the watchman at our school. In the past, it was always the same older folks, but now there are new faces every year. Each watchman is unique, with different personalities and the way they speak. When I was in 10th grade, there was a watchman who went above and beyond to help us. He would carry our bags, buy candy for the kids who were crying, and he makes sure we crossed the road safely. However, when we moved up to 11th grade, we saw a new watchman who remained silent throughout the day. He would sit by the door, opening and closing it without saying a word. We never see him open his mouth to speak. This year, a new watchman arrived, and he was constantly shouting and scolding everyone to walk quickly. He had an angry face all day, and we were more afraid of him than our teachers," she said and asked him, "Should we treat them all with equal respect?"

"Maybe not," he said.

"Looking back, I realized that each watchman had a different impact on our school experience. While some were kind and helpful, others were strict and unapproachable. For the last watchman, his profession and his age deserve respect, but not his character. Then how to balance the respect towards him," she asked.

"Respect is not something that can be earned by force or by position. It is something that has to be earned by qualities, abilities and character. Everyone deserves to be treated with respect, regardless of their background and position. You should be aware of power dynamics and avoid any behavior that could be seen as disrespectful or unfair. It's important to remember that everyone we encounter has their own story and struggles. We should treat everyone with respect and kindness, regardless of their role or position, to create a positive and inclusive environment. As you said, only his age and profession deserve respect. That doesn't mean you have to disrespect him," he said.

"So should I respect him in the way I respect the remaining two?" she asked.

"There is no compulsion for you to respect him. You may find it easier to just stay away from him and not mind him anymore than dis-respecting him," he said.

"When it comes to parents?" she asked.

"Look Deesha, Respect is important regardless of who the person is. There is a common assumption that all parents are inherently good, but the reality is that there are many who fall short of this expectation. But your dad is really a good guy. From some perspective, he thinks that making you wait for a year is acceptable. If you want to prove him wrong, make him understand your needs in a calm way. He is not a random watchman to pull him out of your life," he said.

Deesha had a smile on her face and asked him, "Can you speak to him?"

"Yeah, I will," he said.

"Okay. I can't fight or argue a lot with them. I don't want to see them hurt," she said.

"If you're fighting or arguing for good things, you should fight for a long span," he said, and asked her, "If you fought hard with them to travel to the town for education, and accomplished your goals - would your parents feel happy about?"

"Of course yes," she said.

"Your mom is getting better, I don't know why your dad is making you wait," he said.

"That remains a mystery," she said.

"You go home and have some rest. I'll talk to your dad in the evening," he assured.

The old man could sense why Tilak asked Deesha to pause her studies for a year. To make sure his intuition was right, he decided to meet Tilak at dusk. After Deesha left, the old man tied the cattle under the shadow and took some rest.

Hours passed, and the sun was gone. He woke up and all of a sudden, he started coughing intensely. He went near the pot and had some water, but the cough persisted for a few minutes. He went to his bed and sat on it again. After a few seconds, the cough subsided. While having a coughing fit, he grabbed a towel to muffle the sound, but upon closer inspection, he saw some spots of blood on it. He knew that he was getting older and older and this blood stain wasn't a big deal compared to the tragedies in his past. He took a while and headed to Deesha's house. The door was already open when he reached it. He knocked on it and Deesha came out.

"Is your dad home?" he asked.

"Yeah, he is having a shower," she said.

"Why don't you join us for dinner? Let's dine together," Sradha asked as she stepped outside.

Following his shower, Tilak had a quick chat with the old man, and the four of them had their dinner. Three of them had some fun conversation and Deesha seemed silent. The old man felt like he had never seen her this way. After completing his dinner, the old man said to Tilak and Sradha, "I need to have a conversation about Deesha."

"About her higher studies?" Tilak asked.

"Yes. Can we step out and speak about this?" the old man asked.

Tilak had a soft gaze towards Deesha, who was still consuming her dinner. "Yeah, come," Tilak said to the old man.

"She's deeply concerned about the situation. Nevertheless, her desire to go to town for her studies remains strong. At least you guys should understand her. She tries to avoid any arguments that might hurt you both," the old man said.

"To be honest, I'm the first one who wants her to go to town for her studies. Over the course of last twelve months, Sradha's medical expenses had a big impact on my savings. That's the main reason I'm asking her to wait for a year. I can't tell her about my financial situation, that's why I told her mom's health as a concern," Tilak said.

The old man's intuition was correct, as he suspected that Tilak's financial struggles were making Deesha wait for a year. His intuition was accurate. So he told them, "Don't worry about the money. We can manage."

"No please, I'm already not okay with you working on the farm. We can't give you so much burden," Sradha said.

"Yes. we won't," Tilak said.

"Listen, upon awakening in this village under a tree, I was initially unaware of how I ended up there.

The very next day, I found a letter in my bag and someone had written that I was from a post-momentary memory loss. The guy who wrote that letter left some money in my bag, which belongs to me. That money still remains untouched. I have no use of that, so we can use it for her studies," the old man said.

"No, we can't do that. Don't force us," Sradha said.

Tilak remained silent and the old man told them, "If you're feeling uneasy, you have the right to return my money at your convenience. So don't pause her studies."

Sradha and Tilak had a look at each other, and she was still uncomfortable about it. After a few seconds, Tilak said, "Okay we'll take that. But I can't leave Sradha alone in the house for 2 days."

"Don't worry, I've been in the town before. I will take her. Just don't mention that I'm helping her with funds," the old man said.

Tilak and Sradha felt thankful to the old man for everything he did. The old man went near the house and told Deesha, "We're going to the town."

Overcome with joy, she sprinted towards her father and embraced him tightly. Both Sradha and Tilak were teasing Deesha a lot. Putting up a grin and a shake of his head, the old man smiled at Tilak and Sradha. With a good night to the trio, he turned and made his way back to the farm and had a sleep.

After a week had gone by, Deesha finished her final exams. It's just one night away until she sets off on her journey to the town. The old man's cough worsened progressively as time went on. He was not even interested in diagnosing it. Whenever he goes through a negative phase of his life, he begins to suffer from the trauma of his losses. Deesha asked him to pack enough clothes for three days. But the old man packed all his clothes. The journey is approximately 400 kilometers, and it could take up to 5 to 6 hours to reach the town. Tilak ensured that their travel plans were sorted by arranging tickets and purchasing an additional return ticket for the old man. As he got to travel a long time, he felt it was important for him to rest up. He went to his bed, and the wind was relentless. After struggling with the wind for quite a time, he fell asleep.

The golden rays of the morning sun illuminated the sky. With a happy expression, he did the monotonous routine to the cattle before preparing for the journey. He took his bag and started walking towards Deesha's house. She had everything ready and was waiting for him at her doorstep. Tilak was advising her a lot and the old man could see it. After the old man came, he had some words with Tilak and Sradha, got some cash, and asked Deesha, "Shall we go?"

She said, "Yes," to the old man, and she told her parents, "I know it's tough to see me go, but you both should promise to meet me once in a every month."

Sradha was unable to speak, her eyes were filled with tears. Tilak holding back his emotions, reassured Deesha, "Yes, we definitely will."

After bidding a wave to her parents, she started walking with the old man.

"It looks like your dad has filled you with lots of advice," the old man asked.

"Yes, a lot," she replied.

"What did he say?" he asked.

"Should stay respectful to others, eat well, limit unnecessary outdoor activities, post letters to them regularly, and most importantly, refrain from making inappropriate jokes," she said.

"I think your dad is afraid of your jokes, more than leaving you alone in the town," he said with a laugh.

Both had a smile and headed to the nearby train station. Both of them were blabbering and having some fun conversations while heading. After they reached the train station, the old man ensured that Deesha had everything she needed for her journey. Once aboard the train, they made their way to their coach and took their seats. Since it was a middle of the week, the coach was devoid of passengers. So they took a seat facing each other.

As the train started moving, the old man gazed out through the window while Deesha watched him intently, never taking her eyes off him. The old man noticed it and asked her, "You wanna ask something?"

"Why are you helping us?" she asked.

"I don't know," he said.

"If you don't mind, I have a question to ask," she said.

"Yeah, go on," he said with curiosity.

"You haven't told me about your kids. Haven't you?" she asked.

"No. I don't have kids," he replied.

"Everything about you sounds abnormal. It's not common to meet someone without kids. Can you tell me the reason?" she asked.

"There's no significant reason to shed light on it extensively. My wife and I decided not to have any," he said.

"Could you please tell me about your wife," she asked.

"You wanna listen to my love story," he asked with a smile.

"Why not?" she said.

"Yes. You can," he replied.

A rosy tint began to spread across his cheeks, causing Deesha to grin in amusement. He started having a smile on his face for putting himself in this situation. Suddenly, it started raining outside and the sky turned grey within a few seconds. The window was shut to keep the rain from getting inside. The chillness began to fill the compartment, and it stimulated his senses to tell about his romantic story. As no one was inside this compartment except them, he felt free to share. He started to explain about his lady.

Love is Both Intellectual and Heartful

"Understanding the intricacies of love might be a challenge for many. But when we start unfolding every knot, it will lead us to a unique and memorable experience. According to popular belief, true love is a once-in-a-lifetime occurrence. Honestly, it's not true. We humans have been living every minute of our lives in different aspects and understandings. As people live with different understandings, each person has a unique universe in their head. When we meet people with different understandings, we'll get new experiences. Basically, women possess an enchanting ability to work wonders in the lives of others. Like the queen on the chess board," the old man said.

"Queen on the chess board?" she asked with a doubt.

"Yes. The Queen holds a special place as the most powerful piece, with the ability to move in any direction. Similarly, women hold a unique place in society, with the magical ability to transform the lives of those around them. With their empathy and emotional intelligence, women can make a profound impact on others lives, providing unwavering emotional support and covering every black and white box of life with care and compassion. So, just like the Queen in the game of chess, women hold incredible power to make a positive difference in the world. This works with both the women I met," the old man said.

"You married twice?" she asked.

"No, I was yet to marry the first woman, but she met with an accident, and she…," the old man struggled to say.

Deesha understood his emotions and all of a sudden, she said, "Yeah, I know. Don't stress."

"Let me tell you about the person I married," he said.

As the rain intensified, the breezy atmosphere inside became even more inviting and he began to recount his story.

After the passing of my first love, I placed myself in quarantine. I shut myself away from the world, and even when I did venture out, I kept my emotions locked away. During that time, nothing seemed to make sense to me. I spent my days alone, lost in the pages of novels. It was through these novels that I was able to find some solace and engagement, as the stories drew me in and allowed me to escape my own pain for a while.

After 4 years of losing my first love, one day, I was searching for a book at the nearest library and I noticed a woman doing the same. She was in a purple outfit and her hair was in a cascade of waves, like strands of silk spun by a master weaver. That's where I met her first time. Later, I was looking at the description of a book and we exchanged a few glances but kept to ourselves. The almond shape of her eyes gave her a magical allure, while the depth of its hue hinted at a mysterious soul. After a few minutes, she came near me and struck up a conversation with a low tone. She said she was familiar with the book I was reading. Despite my usual discomfort in social situations, she made me feel at ease and soon we chatted like old friends. Maybe the ambience of the library made me comfortable. I don't know how, but she made me speak a lot. We shared a mutual love for the author and the books. Our conversations continued every Saturday, and we discovered our shared passion for reading. As we delved deeper into each other's lives, we found ourselves drawn to each other, unsure of where this bond would take us. Honestly, we don't even know we are falling in love.

Saturday meets became a daily meet. With each shared smile and stolen glance, an unspoken connection grew between us. Eventually, she mustered up the courage to ask me out for a coffee and I invited her home. From the moment she stepped into my house, she started listening to my pain and tragic past until the coffee we were drinking went cold. She won my heart over completely when she treated me with the utmost care and tenderness, like a precious piece of art amidst the chaos.

She understood me in a way that no one else ever did. Each and every day, I spoke to her about the grief I had after my first love's passing. She listened patiently and never judged me for my worries. As we spent more time together, I realized that we had a lot in common. We both had a deep appreciation for art and literature, and we bonded over our shared love for them. What started as a common interest, but soon blossomed into a beautiful relationship. The thing that struck me the most about her was her ability to see beyond my flaws and accept me for who I am. With her by my side, I felt like I could overcome any obstacle. Our connection was so strong that we created our own little world, where our problems didn't matter and our unique bond was all that we needed.

One of the best things I learned from her is, love is not just emotional, but also intellectual. It is a complex and multifaceted experience that involves the heart, mind, and soul. Love involves a combination of intellectual stimulation and emotional connection, shared values, and a deep understanding of each other's needs and desires. - the old man said.

"I was lost in your story. It sounds beautiful," Deesha said with a smile on her face.

"I cherish every moment that I spent with her, and I know that she will always be an irreplaceable part of my life," his eyes were wet with tears as he spoke, reflecting his strong feelings.

The old man's coughing fits seemed to worsen. Concerned, Deesha asked if he was okay, but he quickly changed the subject. They continued to chat, enjoying each other's company and sharing jokes until they were both out of breath from laughing. It was 10 am, but due to the greyish tone of the sky, it looked like 7 pm. However, with each kilometer they crossed, the clouds cleared, and the sun shone brighter. After realizing the amount of workload that awaiting them in town, they opted to take a break. Deesha couldn't sleep well last night due to her anticipation about going to town, and now she drifted off to sleep. The old man was looking out through the window, and the memories of his late wife flooded his mind.

Hours passed, and the train arrived at its destination. The old man gently woke Deesha and helped her gather their luggage. They stepped out onto the platform, and immediately Deesha felt the weight of her parent's absence. She knew that once the old man leaves her, she would be truly alone. The old man looked at her face and asked, "Are you missing your parents already?"

Deesha replied in a monotone voice, "Yes, terribly."

As they made their way towards the exit of the train station, the old man turned to Deesha and spoke to her in a gentle tone. "You don't have to worry, my dear. Remember what your father uttered - he'll pay a visit every month to see you," he said.

"I haven't left them alone for this long before," she said.

It's important to familiarize yourself with these emotions, as doing so will improve your life," he said.

She remained silent. The old man went to a store nearby and asked about the location of the institute. Hopefully, it's just a walkable distance, and they started walking towards it. Eventually, they arrived at the institute, and Deesha went inside to speak with some people. The old man waited outside for an hour until Deesha returned and shared the news with him, "They've asked me to come back tomorrow. So, we can go to a hostel."

"We should search for a better one," he said.

"No need to search. The institute provided me with one," she said.

" That's great," he said.

Deesha remained dull as they made their way to the hostel. Despite the old man's attempts to lift her spirits, she remained unresponsive. Once they reached the hostel, the old man signed in as Deesha's guardian in the hostel entry book. Deesha tried to decode his name from his signature, but it was unintelligible. The old man then took Deesha and her luggage to the gate but had to leave her there as it is a women's hostel.

Deesha checked into the room, settled her luggage, and freshened up before rejoining the old man for a conversation. As time went by, he stepped out of the hostel and settled on a bench outside a nearby cafe. From her room window, Deesha could see him clearly and it reminded her of their conversations a year ago at a store in her village. She started missing him and felt like she wants to complete her studies and do something for him. As night drew closer, she went to bed.

The old man was lost in thought, pondering something crucial. He felt like he had endured all the sorrows a person could face in a lifetime, starting from his childhood. He had been haunted by a question for years - why was his life so tragic? But unfortunately, the answer always eluded him. Every time he tried to make sense of all, his mental health deteriorated. To make matters worse, he was now coughing up blood, and the prospect of redemption in life seemed like a far-off dream for a man like him. He understands that he can't die on that farm and he shouldn't cause any agony or guilt to Deesha and her family. So he decided to go somewhere after making sure all set for Deesha.

Farewell Forever…

He stayed up all night, and the sun crept over the horizon. He waited for Deesha to come out of the hostel and together they made their way to her institute. The old man helped her with the paperwork and it took a whole day at her institute. They strolled back towards her hostel and there was a restaurant nearby caught their eyes. They savored their dishes, lost in the flavors until Deesha questioned him about his return ticket.

"Is your return ticket safe?" she asked

He suddenly turned silent and did not answer her question.

"I'm asking you. Could please react, Mister?" she asked.

She took the water bottle and tapped it on the table. He saw her and took the return ticket from his pocket and kept it on the table.

"Keep it safe," she said.

"No use of this ticket, I'm not going back to your village," he said.

"Stop kidding," she said.

He squeezed his ticket and tossed it away. Deesha was taken aback, demanding to know why.

He didn't want to make her worry about his illness, so he merely stated that he needed a break. "You know right, I was not feeling mentally well for the past 10 to 12 months," he said.

"Yeah, I know. But where do you wanna go to fix that?" she asked.

" I don't know, but I need a break," he stated.

Despite her attempts to persuade him to return to her village, he remained firm in his decision to take a break. After a lengthy argument, he assured her that he would return to her farm, but only after he had sorted himself out.

She finished her meal, unaware of his lies. As they walked back to her hostel, little did she know it would be the last time she'd walk with him.

"It's not okay for me to let you go," she said, but she got even more frustrated by his silence. When they arrived at the hostel, he tried to convince her to understand.

"Deesha, I don't usually share my story with just anyone. Surprisingly, I opened up to you. You understand me like no one else could in this phase of my life. I enjoy spending the day under the tree watching your cattle, but mentally, I'm not okay. I need time to regain my strength," he explained.

Deesha understands him and his situation, telling him to stay strong and careful wherever he goes.

With a whole heart, she said, "I felt happy and gained a lot of knowledge whenever I had a chat with you. I'm standing here, under the strong yellowish street light, somewhere around 400 kilometers away from my house. You're the reason for it and you made this possible. With your help, I'm gonna kick start a new journey from tomorrow. I don't know how long will you take to come back, but I'll wait for you from the next moment you leave."

The old man scratched Deesha's head and said, "You'll be successful one day."

"One more time, I'd love to hear your thoughts about life, and learn from them, like I usually do," she asked him.

"What do you wanna know about?" he asked.

"Anything," she said.

"Anything or everything," he asked her with a smile.

A small grin appeared on her face as she realized he was asking her the same question she had asked him a year ago.

"Everything," she said.

The old man gave his final piece of advice to her.

In our society, there's this popular belief that success is guaranteed by studying hard. While education is certainly important for financial support, true success lies in developing your life experience and ideologies alongside your studies. Facing adversity and learning from it can give you a better understanding of life. It's crucial to form clear and good opinions about the problems that exist in our society.

Be it love, a job, or even a competition, no matter who sheds tears, try hard with determination and passion until achieving your needs, if it's truly good and right. While it doesn't matter whether you succeed or not, just try.

Great leaders have always been a source of inspiration and guidance for people all over the world. Nelson Mandela, Dr. B.R. Ambedkar, Frederick Douglass, and Mother Teresa are some of the most revered personalities in history. While it's natural to want to follow them, it's important to remember that they were also humans, with their own flaws and shortcomings. Rather than idolizing them completely and carrying their good and bad in our own heads, it's better to focus on the principles that made them great and incorporate them into our own lives. By doing so, we can learn from their successes and failures, and create our own path to success while staying true to our values and beliefs.

Don't join in the group that divides people into different factions.

As I said earlier, this world has changed everything and everyone in a competitive way. People started prioritizing money in front of everything. These days, money has the ability to buy a job, win a competition, and even it can buy love. However, in such a world, if you get a chance to achieve these things without the help of money, you're living a real life and you're succeeding in it.

Even if you have faith in God, even if you go up and down thousands of God's shrines, some sins will not be forgiven. We can avoid any sin by refraining from intruding into other people's personal lives, by treating everyone's emotions with respect, and by avoiding any form of discrimination and typecasting. By living our lives in this way, we can ensure that we do not cause harm to others.

Deesha understood everything he said and nodded her head. With a voice full of sorrow, she asked him, "So you're going now?"

The old man remained silent and scratched her head again. She was already missing her parents and after his decision, the ache in her heart grew stronger as she realized that she was now on her own.

As he asked her to enter the hostel, he turned back and began to walk away. It was a painfully slow walk that seemed to last an eternity for her, and she couldn't help but feel her eyes welling up with tears. She knew that he was about to disappear from her sight in mere moments and she found herself shouting at him, "Wait! You haven't even told me your name yet!"

The old man walked on looking back at Deesha and said, "I'll tell you soon."

Within a few seconds. He faded from her eyes.

Present Day…

As Deesha clutching her champagne glass with tears streaming down her face, on the other side, her parents fixed their eyes on the door, waiting for the old man to return, so they could give him back his money and love. But deep down, they knew that it was a false hope, and Deesha knew it too.

As time passed, the truth sank in, and Deesha realized that the old man was gone. With a heavy heart, she put down her glass and made a promise to herself that she would never forget the lesson that the old man had taught her - that true success is not measured by money or caste/ community/religion/ and race, but by the impact we have on others lives.

Life goes on…..

Someday Perhaps

www.ingramcontent.com/pod-product-compliance
Lightning Source LLC
Chambersburg PA
CBHW021226130726
47988CB00002B/835